THIS BLOOMSBURY BOOK

BELONGS TO

First published in Great Britain in
2002 by Bloomsbury Publishing Plc
38 Soho Square, London, W1D 3HB
This paperback edition first published in 2004

Illustrations copyright © Lorna Hussey 2002
The moral right of the illustrator has been asserted

A CIP catalogue record of this book is available from the British Library
ISBN 0 7475 5019 0

Printed and bound by South China Printing Co

1 3 5 7 9 10 8 6 4 2

All papers used by Bloomsbury Publishing are natural,
recyclable products made from wood grown in well-managed
forests. The manufacturing processes conform to the
environmental regulations of the
country of origin.

NONSENSE VERSE

by LEWIS CARROLL

Illustrations by
LORNA HUSSEY

BLOOMSBURY
CHILDREN'S
BOOKS

THE MOCK TURTLE'S SONG

'Will you walk a little faster,' said a whiting to a snail,
'There's a porpoise close behind me, and he's treading on my tail.
See how eagerly the lobsters and the turtles all advance!
They are waiting on the shingle – will you come and join the dance?'
Will you, won't you, will you, won't you, will you join the dance?
Will you, won't you, will you, won't you, won't you join the dance?

'You can really have no notion how delightful it will be
When they take us up and throw us, with the lobsters, out to sea!'
But the snail replied, 'Too far, too far!' and gave a look askance –
Said he thanked the whiting kindly, but he would not join the dance.
Would not, could not, would not, could not, would not join the dance.
Would not, could not, would not, could not, could not join the dance.

'What matters it how far we go?' his scaly friend replied.
'There is another shore, you know, upon the other side.
The further off from England the nearer is to France –
Then turn not pale, beloved snail, but come and join the dance.'
Will you, won't you, will you, won't you, will you join the dance?
Will you, won't you, will you, won't you, won't you join the dance?

JABBERWOCKY

'Twas brillig, and the slithy toves
    Did gyre and gimble in the wabe;
All mimsy were the borogroves,
    And the mome raths outgrabe.

'Beware the Jabberwock, my son!
    The jaws that bite, the claws that catch!
Beware the Jubjub bird, and shun
    The frumious Bandersnatch!'

He took his vorpal sword in hand:
    Long time the manxome foe he sought –
So rested he by the Tumtum tree,
    And stood awhile in thought.

And as in uffish thought he stood,
    The Jabberwock, with eyes of flame,
Came whiffling through the tulgey wood,
    And burbled as it came!

One, two! One, two! And through and through
    The vorpal blade went snicker-snack!
He left it dead, and with its head
    He went galumphing back.

'And hast thou slain the Jabberwock?
    Come to my arms, my beamish boy!
O frabjous day! Callooh! Callay!'
    He chortled in his joy.

'Twas brillig, and the slithy toves
    Did gyre and gimble in the wabe;
All mimsy were the borogroves,
    And the mome raths outgrabe.

THE KING FISHER'S SONG

King Fisher courted Lady Bird –
Sing Beans, sing Bones, sing Butterflies!
'Find me my match,' he said,
'With such a noble head –
With such a beard, as white as curd –
With such expressive eyes!'

'Yet pins have heads,' said Lady Bird –
Sing Prunes, sing Prawns, sing Primrose Hill!
'And, where you stick them in,
They stay, and thus a pin
Is very much to be preferred
To one that's never still!'

'Oysters have beards,' said Lady Bird –
Sing Flies, sing Frogs, sing Fiddle-strings!
'I love them, for I know
They never chatter so:
They would not say one single word –
Not if you crowned them Kings!'

'Needles have eyes!' said Lady Bird –
Sing Cats, sing Corks, sing Cowslip tea!
'And they are sharp – just what
Your Majesty is *not*.
So get you gone – 'tis too absurd
To come a-courting *me*!'

THE THREE BADGERS

There be three Badgers on a mossy stone,
    Beside a dark and covered way:
Each dreams himself a monarch on his throne,
    And so they stay and stay –
Though their old Father languishes alone,
    They stay, and stay, and stay.

There be three Herrings loitering around,
    Longing to share that mossy seat:
Each Herring tries to sing what she has found
    That makes Life seem so sweet.
Thus, with a grating and uncertain sound,
    They bleat, and bleat, and bleat.

The Mother-Herring, on the salt sea-wave,
    Sought vainly for her absent ones:
The Father-Badger, writhing in a cave,
    Shrieked out, 'Return, my sons!
You shall have buns,' he shrieked, 'if you'll behave!
    Yea, buns, and buns, and buns!'

'I fear,' said she, 'your sons have gone astray?
    My daughters left me while I slept.'
'Yes'm,' the Badger said: 'it's as you say.
    They should be better kept.'
Thus the poor parents talked the time away,
    And wept, and wept, and wept.

THE HERRINGS' SONG

'Oh, dear beyond our dearest dreams,
    Fairer than all that fairest seems!
    To feast the rosy hours away,
    To revel in a roundelay!
      How blest would be
      A life so free –
    Ipwergis-Pudding to consume,
    And drink the subtle Azzigoom!'

The Badgers did not care to talk to Fish:
    They did not dote on Herrings' songs:
They never had experienced the dish
    To which that name belongs:
'And oh, to pinch their tails' (this was their wish)
    'With tongs, yea, tongs, and tongs!'

'And are not these the Fish,' the Eldest sighed,
    'Whose Mother dwells beneath the foam?'
'They *are* the Fish!' the Second one replied.
    'And they have left their home!'
'Oh, wicked fish,' the Youngest Badger cried,
    'To roam, yea, roam, and roam!'

Gently the Badgers trotted to the shore –
    The sandy shore that fringed the bay:
Each in his mouth a living Herring bore –
    Those aged ones waxed gay:
Clear rang their voices through the ocean's roar,
    'Hooray, hooray, hooray!'

FATHER WILLIAM

'You are old, Father William,' the young man said,
　　'And your hair has become very white;
And yet you incessantly stand on your head –
　　Do you think, at your age, it is right?'

'In my youth,' Father William replied to his son,
　　'I feared it might injure the brain;
But, now that I'm perfectly sure I have none,
　　Why, I do it again and again.'

'You are old,' said the youth, 'as I mentioned before,
　　And have grown most uncommonly fat;
Yet you turned a back-somersault in at the door –
　　Pray, what is the reason of that?'

'In my youth,' said the sage, as he shook his grey locks,
　　'I kept all my limbs very supple
By the use of this ointment – one shilling the box –
　　Allow me to sell you a couple?'

'You are old,' said the youth, 'and your jaws are too weak
    For anything tougher than suet;
Yet you finished the goose, with the bones and the beak –
    Pray, how did you manage to do it?'

'In my youth,' said his father, 'I took to the law,
    And argued each case with my wife;
And the muscular strength, which it gave to my jaw
    Has lasted the rest of my life.'

'You are old,' said the youth, 'one would hardly suppose
    That your eye was as steady as ever;
Yet you balanced an eel on the end of your nose –
    What made you so awfully clever?'

'I have answered three questions, and that is enough,'
    Said his father. 'Don't give yourself airs!
Do you think I can listen all day to such stuff?
    Be off, or I'll kick you downstairs!'

THE MAD HATTER'S SONG

Twinkle, twinkle, little bat!
How I wonder what you're at!
Up above the world you fly,
Like a tea-tray in the sky.
Twinkle, twinkle –

THE LOBSTER

'Tis the voice of the Lobster: I heard him declare,
'You have baked me too brown, I must sugar my hair.'
As a duck with its eyelids, so he with his nose
Trims his belt and his buttons, and turns out his toes.

I passed by his garden, and marked, with one eye,
How the Owl and the Oyster were sharing a pie;
While the Duck and the Dodo, the Lizard and Cat,
Were swimming in milk round the brim of a hat.

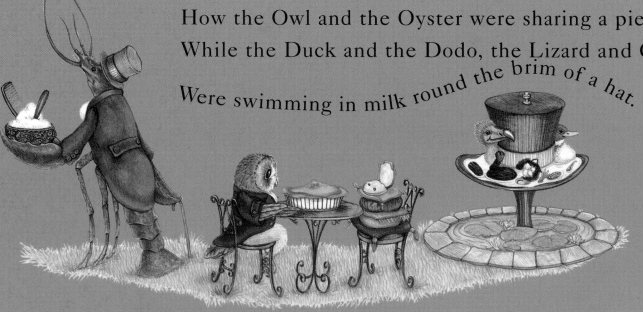

from MELODIES

There was once a young man of Oporta
Who daily got shorter and shorter,
The reason he said
Was the hod on his head,
Which was filled with the heaviest mortar.

His sister named Lucy O'Finner,
Grew constantly thinner and thinner,
The reason was plain,
She slept out in the rain,
And was never allowed any dinner.

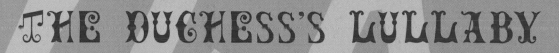

THE DUCHESS'S LULLABY

Speak roughly to your little boy,
And beat him when he sneezes:
He only does it to annoy,
Because he knows it teases.

CHORUS
Wow! wow! wow!

I speak severely to my boy,
I beat him when he sneezes;
For he can thoroughly enjoy
The pepper when he pleases!

CHORUS
Wow! wow! wow!

HUMPTY DUMPTY'S SONG

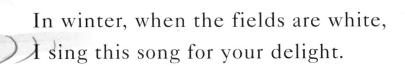

In winter, when the fields are white,
I sing this song for your delight.

In spring, when woods are getting green,
I'll try and tell you what I mean.

In summer, when the days are long,
Perhaps you'll understand the song.

In autumn, when the leaves are brown,
Take pen and ink, and write it down.

I sent a message to the fish:
I told them, 'This is what I wish.'

The little fishes of the sea,
They sent an answer back to me.

The little fishes' answer was,
'We cannot do it, Sir, because—'

I sent to them again to say,
'It will be better to obey.'

The fishes answered, with a grin,
'Why, what a temper you are in!'

I told them once, I told them twice:
They would not listen to advice.

I took a kettle large and new,
Fit for the deed I had to do.

My heart went hop, my heart went thump:
I filled the kettle at the pump.

Then someone came to me and said,
'The little fishes are in bed.'

I said to him, I said it plain,
'Then you must wake them up again.'

I said it very loud and clear:
I went and shouted in his ear.

But he was very stiff and proud:
He said, 'You needn't shout so loud!'

And he was very proud and stiff:
He said, 'I'd go and wake them, if—'

I took a corkscrew from the shelf:
I went to wake them up myself.

And when I found the door was locked,
I pulled and pushed and kicked and knocked.

And when I found the door was shut,
I tried to turn the handle, but—

LITTLE BIRDS

Little Birds are sleeping
All among the pins,
Where the loser wins:
Where, I say, he sneezes,
When and how he pleases –
So the Tale begins.

Little Birds are dining
Warily and well
Hid in mossy cell:
Hid, I say, by waiters
Gorgeous in their gaiters –
I've a Tale to tell.

Little Birds are writing
Interesting books,
To be read by cooks;
Read, I say, not roasted –
Letterpress, when toasted,
Loses its good looks.

Little Birds are feeding
Justices with jam,
Rich in frizzled ham:
Rich, I say, in oysters –
Haunting shady cloisters –
That is what I am.

Little Birds are seeking
Hecatombs of haws,
Dressed in snowy gauze:
Dressed, I say, in fringes
Half-alive with hinges –
Thus they break the laws.

Little Birds are teaching
Tigresses to smile,
Innocent of guile:
Smile, I say, not smirkle –
Mouth a semicircle,
That's the proper style!

Little Birds are playing
Bagpipes on the Shore,
Where the tourists snore:
'Thanks!' they cry. ''Tis thrilling.
Take, oh, take this shilling!
Let us have no more!'

Little Birds are hiding
Crimes in carpet-bags,
Blessed by happy stags:
Blessed, I say, though beaten –
Since our friends are eaten
When the memory flags.

Little Birds are bathing
Crocodiles in cream,
Like a happy dream:
Like, but not so lasting –
Crocodiles, when fasting,
Are not all they seem!

Little Birds are tasting
Gratitude and gold,
Pale with sudden cold;
Pale, I say, and wrinkled –
When the bells have tinkled,
And the Tale is told.

Little Birds are choking
Baronets with bun,
Taught to fire a gun:
Taught, I say, to splinter
Salmon in the winter –
Merely for the fun.

THE WHITE KNIGHT'S BALLAD

I'll tell thee everything I can;
There's little to relate.
I saw an aged aged man,
A-sitting on a gate.
'Who are you, aged man?' I said.
'And how is it you live?'
And his answer trickled through my head
Like water through a sieve.

But I was thinking of a plan
To dye one's whiskers green,
And always use so large a fan
That they could not be seen.
So, having no reply to give
To what the old man said,
I cried, 'Come, tell me how you live!'
And thumped him on the head.

He said, 'I look for butterflies
That sleep among the wheat:
I make them into mutton-pies,
And sell them in the street.
I sell them unto men,' he said,
'Who sail on stormy seas;
And that's the way I get my bread –
A trifle, if you please.'

His accents mild took up the tale:
He said, 'I go my ways,
And when I find a mountain-rill,
I set it in a blaze;
And thence they make a stuff they call
Rowland's Macassar Oil –
Yet twopence-halfpenny is all
They give me for my toil.'

But I was thinking of a way
To feed oneself on batter,
And so go on from day to day
Getting a little fatter.
I shook him well from side to side,
Until his face was blue:
'Come, tell me how you live,' I cried,
'And what it is you do!'

He said, 'I hunt for haddocks' eyes
Among the heather bright,
And work them into waistcoat-buttons
In the silent night.
And these I do not sell for gold
Or coin of silvery shine,
But for a copper halfpenny,
And that will purchase nine.

'I sometimes dig for buttered rolls,
Or set limed twigs for crabs;
I sometimes search the grassy knolls
For wheels of hansom-cabs.
And that's the way' (he gave a wink)
'By which I get my wealth –
And very gladly will I drink
Your Honour's noble health.'

I heard him then, for I had just
Completed my design
To keep the Menai bridge from rust
By boiling it in wine.
I thanked him much for telling me
The way he got his wealth.
But chiefly for his wish that he
Might drink my noble health.

And now, if e'er by chance I put

My fingers into glue,

Or madly squeeze a right-hand foot

Into a left-hand shoe

Or if I drop upon my toe

A very heavy weight,

I weep, for it reminds me so

Of that old man I used to know –

Whose look was mild,

whose speech was slow,

Whose hair was whiter than the snow,

Whose face was very like a crow,

With eyes, like cinders, all aglow,

Who seemed distracted with his woe,

Who rocked his body to and fro,

And muttered mumblingly and low,

As if his mouth were full of dough,

Who snorted like a buffalo –

That summer evening long ago

A-sitting on a gate.

THE WALRUS AND THE CARPENTER

'The sun was shining on the sea,
Shining with all his might:
He did his very best to make
The billows smooth and bright –
And this was odd, because it was
The middle of the night.

The moon was shining sulkily,
Because she thought the sun
Had got no business to be there
After the day was done –
"It's very rude of him," she said,
"To come and spoil the fun!"

The sea was wet as wet could be,
The sands were dry as dry.
You could not see a cloud, because
No cloud was in the sky:
No birds were flying overhead –
There were no birds to fly.

The Walrus and the Carpenter
Were walking close at hand;
They wept like anything to see
Such quantities of sand:
"If this were only cleared away,"
They said, "it would be grand!"

"If seven maids with seven mops
Swept it for half a year,
Do you suppose," the Walrus said,
"That they could get it clear?"
"I doubt it," said the Carpenter,
And shed a bitter tear.

"O Oysters, come and walk with us!"
The Walrus did beseech.
"A pleasant walk, a pleasant talk,
Along the briny beach:
We cannot do with more than four,
To give a hand to each."

The eldest Oyster looked at him.
But never a word he said:
The eldest Oyster winked his eye,
And shook his heavy head –
Meaning to say he did not choose
To leave the oyster-bed.

But four young Oysters hurried up,
All eager for the treat:
Their coats were brushed, their faces washed,
Their shoes were clean and neat –
And this was odd, because, you know,
They hadn't any feet.

Four other Oysters followed them,
And yet another four;
And thick and fast they came at last,
And more, and more and more –
All hopping through the frothy waves,
And scrambling to the shore.

The Walrus and the Carpenter
Walked on a mile or so,
And then they rested on a rock
Conveniently low:
And all the little Oysters stood
And waited in a row.

"The time has come," the Walrus said,
"To talk of many things:
Of shoes – and ships – and sealing-wax –
Of cabbages – and kings –
And why the sea is boiling hot –
And whether pigs have wings."

"But wait a bit," the Oysters cried,
"Before we have our chat;
For some of us are out of breath,
And all of us are fat!"
"No hurry!" said the Carpenter.
They thanked him much for that.

"A loaf of bread," the Walrus said,
"Is what we chiefly need:
Pepper and vinegar besides
Are very good indeed –
Now if you're ready, Oysters dear,
We can begin to feed."

"But not on us!" the Oysters cried,
Turning a little blue.
"After such kindness, that would be
A dismal thing to do!"
"The night is fine," the Walrus said.
"Do you admire the view?

"It was so kind of you to come!
And you are very nice!"
The Carpenter said nothing but
"Cut us another slice:
I wish you were not quite so deaf –
I've had to ask you twice!"

"It seems a shame," the Walrus said,
"To play them such a trick,
After we've brought them out so far,
And made them trot so quick!"
The Carpenter said nothing but
"The butter's spread too thick!"

"I weep for you," the Walrus said,
"I deeply sympathise."
With sobs and tears he sorted out
Those of the largest size,
Holding his pocket-handkerchief
Before his streaming eyes.

"O Oysters," said the Carpenter.
"You've had a pleasant run!
Shall we be trotting home again?"
But answer came there none –
And this was scarcely odd, because
They'd eaten every one.'